Cactus Coyote

Cactus Coyote

AND OTHER STORIES OF ANIMAL ESCAPADES
Compiled by the Editors
of
Highlights for Children

CONTENTS

Cactus Coyote

By Marianne Mitchell

One bright summer morning, Coyote trotted down a dusty arroyo. As usual, he was hungry. He'd been out all night hunting for his dinner, and all he had found were a few tiny mice. At last, his sharp eyes saw Rabbit dozing under some dry tumbleweeds. His swift paws caught sleepy Rabbit by surprise.

But Rabbit didn't panic. He poked his small fuzzy head out from under Coyote's paws and said, "Mr. Coyote, a great hunter like you deserves a bigger meal than me. I am much too small. Let me go, and I will lead you to my brother's house. He is much fatter."

Coyote looked at the scrawny rabbit in his paws. *One rabbit is good, but two rabbits would be better,* he thought greedily.

"You're right," he said. "You would hardly be a mouthful. And I am very hungry this morning." He put Rabbit down and gave him a shove. "Off you go, then. But no tricks. I am right behind you."

Rabbit scampered across the desert to the big paloverde tree where his brother had a cozy burrow. He jumped in and shouted, "Coyote is coming! We must hide!" So the two rabbits wiggled their way to a deep, dark corner.

This little trick wasn't going to stop Coyote. He knew all about rabbit holes. He looked around until he found the escape hole and pushed a rock over it. Then he started digging. Soon his big, dirty snout was poking the two frightened rabbits.

"Finally, I can have my dinner!" said Coyote. And he ran a long, greedy tongue over his pointy teeth.

But Rabbit was very brave. He raised his paw and said, "Wait, Mr. Coyote! You have worked very hard today. You must be even hungrier now.

Let us go, and we'll lead you to our brother's house. He has spent all summer eating juicy red cactus pears. He's much fatter than we are."

Coyote rubbed his stomach. A three-rabbit stew sounded even better than a two-rabbit stew. He backed away from the two rabbits.

"Off you go, then," said Coyote. "But no tricks. I am right behind you."

The two rabbits zipped through the sagebrush to the home of their big brother. He lived in a hole at the base of a prickly pear cactus.

"Coyote is coming! And he wants a fat rabbit for dinner!" they cried.

"And he shall have one," said their big brother. "Come. We'll fix up a surprise for him."

Near the prickly pear cactus grew another cactus, called teddy bear *cholla*. It looked soft and fuzzy like a teddy bear, but it had long, sharp thorns with little hooks on the ends. Chunks of cholla cactus lay scattered all over the ground. The three rabbits gently pushed together pieces of cholla until they had shaped a huge cactus rabbit.

Coyote arrived and circled around slowly. He peered into the hole at the bottom of the prickly pear cactus, looking for the three rabbits. They were in there, all right. And sitting right next to them was the biggest rabbit he had ever seen.

"Oh, boy!" whispered Coyote. "What a delicious stew this will be!"

He quickly gathered up sticks to make his cook fire. Soon the flames were jumping. The spicy smell of mesquite filled the air.

"Come out, my friends, and sit by my fire. Let me tell you about my adventures," said Coyote.

But the three rabbits stayed where they were.

Coyote's stomach growled. The rabbits huddled closer together.

"Oh, don't be afraid. That's just the sound of distant thunder," said Coyote. He tossed some more sticks on the crackling fire and the smoke billowed up.

Then the three rabbits put their heads together. On the count of ONE . . . TWO . . . THREE! they blew the smoke into Coyote's eyes. The rabbits quickly dashed into the desert.

Coyote sputtered and coughed and rubbed his eyes. As soon as he could, he looked into the cactus again. Three of the rabbits were gone, for sure. But . . . could it be? The biggest rabbit of all was still there!

"No more tricks," he cried. "Now you're mine!" But Coyote was so greedy he forgot to be careful. He shoved his paws into the hole and grabbed the cholla cactus rabbit.

"Yeow! Ow!" Hundreds of spiky thorns pricked Coyote's paws. He kicked and danced. He tried shaking off the cholla. He snapped and chomped. "Yeow! Ow!" But he only got a mouthful of cactus. From his whiskery nose to his long bushy tail, he was covered with cactus.

Coyote no longer thought about rabbits or rabbit stew. He limped down to the river to soak his poor, stickery body. Why couldn't he learn not to be so greedy?

Safe and sound in their new burrow, Rabbit and his brothers sat down to a delicious dinner of prickly pear salad.

"Here's to the little guys!" they cheered.

And off in the distance they heard Coyote crying about his sore body and his lost dinner.

"Ow! Ow! Ow! Owwoooooooooo!"

Peter Pelican's Pouch

By Anita Borgo

The cans of tuna fish from Sam Seal's Oceanside Store clanked together in Peter Pelican's pouch. He waddled along the beach enjoying the salty breeze. Peter usually didn't carry important, useful things like tuna fish in his pouch. He usually carried unimportant, useless things.

"The more unimportant and useless the better," Peter's wife, Penelope, always said.

Each morning Peter strolled the beach, collecting a bit of paper here, a length of rope there, whatever the swimmers and tourists left behind. He gave it all to his clever wife. Then Penelope imagined and thought, snipped and sewed. She made his sunglasses from a cellophane candy wrapper and a bit of wire that washed ashore. She made his sandals from shoelaces and a cracked pail that was buried in the sand. Penelope was a clever pelican.

Peter decided that today he would be clever, too. He would find the most unimportant and useless things he had ever collected and change them somehow, just like Penelope did.

As Peter made his plans, something tickled him. He lifted his sunglasses and looked down. The end of a blue-striped towel flapped in the wind and brushed against his orange legs.

"I can see why no one would want this," Peter said. He shook the dirty, frayed cloth and stuffed it into his pouch. "It's too small and ripped to be a useful towel."

The towel had dirtied Peter's white feathers, and he rinsed himself in the sea. As he thought about how to make a useless towel useful, something bumped him. A wave floated a straw hat into his knobby knees. He scooped up the tattered hat. Water streamed through a large hole in the top.

"I can see why no one wanted this," Peter said. He wrung the water from the hat and shoved it into his pouch. "The brim is bent and the top is worn. It's an unimportant hat."

As Peter hurried home to somehow change the towel and hat into something better and be as clever as Penelope, something stubbed his toe. An empty pickle jar caught his foot, sandal and all. Peter tugged at the glass jar.

"I can see why no one wanted this," Peter said. He scraped off a strand of seaweed that had dried onto its side. Then he carefully packed the jar into his pouch. "With no lid, this is a useless and unimportant jar."

When Peter arrived home, he unpacked his pouch. The frayed towel, tattered hat, and empty jar looked as useless and unimportant as ever. He couldn't figure out how to change them. He could only think of lunch and the tuna fish from Sam Seal's Oceanside Store.

Penelope came in from her flower garden, carrying the rake that she had made from an old umbrella. She spied the towel, hat, and jar. Peter knew she was thinking and imagining already.

"You can have them," Peter said. "I'll never be as clever as you."

Peter mixed the tuna with chopped squid and kelp. Penelope washed and dried the towel. Then she hemmed it into a neat square.

Peter sliced wheat bread into thick slabs. His wife brushed off the straw hat and bent the brim just so.

Peter hunted in the cupboard for a package of seaweed chips to have with their sandwiches. Penelope scrubbed the glass jar until it gleamed. She filled it with water. Then she flew to her garden.

Peter heard her *snip, snip, snip.* Penelope returned with a wingful of poppies, snapdragons, and petunias. She arranged the flowers in the jar and placed the jar in the overturned hat. Then she covered the table with the striped towel and set the hat, jar, and flowers on top of the towel. Last of all, she smiled at Peter.

Peter admired his clever wife, but why couldn't he imagine that the towel could become a table-cloth? Or the jar a vase? Or the hat a basket?

"If I were clever, I could change something and make it useful and important," said Peter.

"You have, Peter," Penelope said. "By collecting each day, you've changed a littered beach into a safe, clean one that everyone enjoys."

Peter thought about that as he and Penelope ate lunch. Afterwards, they strolled along the beach and both of them felt clever.

Tish

By Bonnie Highsmith Taylor

Tish didn't like being a farm cow.

She didn't like getting up early in the morning or grazing in the hot sun all day. She didn't like standing still while Farmer Jenks milked her.

"I want to be big and important," she said.

"You are important to Farmer Jenks," said Queenie, who was the oldest cow on the farm. "And you certainly are big enough."

All the other cows laughed.

"Just you wait," said Tish. "Someday I'll be very big and important."

Day after day Tish complained. "Why do I have to be a plain old farm cow?"

Every morning when Farmer Jenks drove the cows into the barn Tish would moo, "It's too early to get up."

When Farmer Jenks tried to milk her she would step from side to side and swish her tail.

"Please hold still, Tish," Farmer Jenks would plead as he sat beside her.

When Tish followed the other cows to pasture she would grumble, "Why can't I lie in the shade and have someone bring me my food?"

One day a big black car stopped in front of the farm and two men got out.

"There she is!" shouted one man, pointing at Tish. "Just the cow we have been looking for!"

"What a star she would make!" cried the other man. "Let's go talk to the farmer."

Tish felt herself swelling with pride. She held her head high and mooed, "I'm going to be big and important at last."

Later that day the two men came back in a truck and loaded Tish into it.

On and on they drove until they came to a place with a lot of buildings. It looked like the fairgrounds where Tish had won a blue ribbon when she was a calf.

The next thing she knew, she was in a clean, cozy stable. There was sweet alfalfa hay to eat and cool water to drink. In the corner was a nice bed of straw.

One man brushed Tish's coat while another fed her a big juicy apple.

If the other cows could see me now, sighed Tish to herself.

That night she lay down on her soft straw bed. As she closed her eyes she thought, *"Tomorrow I shall sleep until noon."*

But Tish did not sleep until noon! No way!

At the break of day a man came into the stable. "On your feet, girl. The director wants you on the set in ten minutes."

Tish blinked sleepily. *Director? Set? What on earth is that?* she wondered.

Tish soon found out. The set was a place where they made movies, and the director was the person who told everyone what to do.

Tish stumbled about, still half asleep. Everyone was shouting and running around in circles.

"Ready!" shouted the director in a gruff voice "Quiet on the set! Lights!"

Suddenly Tish was blinded by lights coming from every direction. She felt herself growing hotter and hotter.

"This is worse than being out in the hot sun," she mumbled to herself.

Tish shook her head.

"Hold still!" the director shouted.

She swished her tail.

"Tish, hold still!"

All day long she stood under the hot lights trying to be perfectly still.

The next day and the day after that it was the same. She was wakened at daybreak and led on to the hot, noisy set where the director screamed at her until her head was nearly splitting.

Tish thought of all the other cows back on the farm. She thought of Farmer Jenks. How kind and patient he was.

Oh, how she longed to be back home.

An idea popped into Tish's head. She swished her tail up and down and side to side.

"Hold still!" the director shouted.

Tish shook her head.

"Tish, hold still!"

She kicked up her hind legs and bellowed. "MOO! MOO! MOO!"

"Stop that!" shouted the angry director.

But Tish bellowed louder. "MOOOO!"

Around and around the set she ran, kicking over lamps, cameras, and props.

"Get her out of here!" shrieked the director. "Get her out of my sight!"

By that afternoon, Tish was back in the pasture with the other cows.

Tish never complains anymore. She doesn't mind the hot sun. She stands perfectly still while Farmer Jenks milks her. She's the first one awake in the morning.

Soon, Tish is going to have her very own calf.

Every day she tells the other cows, "Mine will be no ordinary calf. Some day it will be very big and important."

The other cows just look at her and shake their heads.

Curious Amos

By Helen Kronberg

Amos sat in front of the snug little cave. He watched the chipmunks chase each other around the oak tree.

"Eat your fish," Mother Bear said.

"I'm not hungry," said Amos. "I want to go and play."

Father Bear grunted. "A bear with any sense would be eating. It's nearly time for our winter sleep. Eat, or you'll be too hungry to sleep."

"I don't want to sleep," said Amos.

"Amos," scolded Mother Bear. "Bears always sleep in winter."

"Why?"

Father Bear growled. "Why. Always why! Why do you always have to know why?"

"Winter is a time of snow and ice," said Mother Bear. "It's not a good time for bears to be out and about. Not good at all."

"Snow? Ice? What does it look like? How does it feel? Does it smell like spring violets or like wet fall leaves?" asked Amos.

Father Bear sniffed the air. "There's already a winter crispness in the air," he said.

Amos raised up and sniffed. Hmmm. It was not like anything he had smelled before.

"Do all animals sleep in winter?" he asked.

"There are foolish animals, like the deer," said Father Bear. "They grow thin from lack of food."

"Is it pretty in winter?" asked Amos. "Does snow taste good? What color is ice?"

Father Bear chuckled. "Curious Amos. Remember the time you stuck your nose in a hollow tree? You were not happy just to gather honey. You had to watch the bees at work. Curiosity got your nose stung."

Amos rubbed his nose. "Does winter feel like bees?" he asked.

Mother Bear sighed. "We don't really know much about winter," she said. "We only know that it's the time when all bears sleep."

Father Bear yawned. "And it's about that time now," he said.

"Not yet," Amos begged. "I don't want to go to sleep yet."

Mother Bear and Father Bear looked at each other and sighed.

"He will be too curious to sleep," said Mother Bear, shaking her head.

"We will lie awake worrying about him," said Father Bear. "But our Amos must learn some hard lessons. When you have seen enough, Amos, come into the cave. We will cuddle up and get you warm."

Amos laughed as snow began to fall. It was beautiful. Why did bears want to miss it?

He ambled through the forest. It was so quiet. Most of the small animals were in their burrows. Even the birds were gone from the trees. He wished he had other bears with whom to share his excitement. But all his friends were snug in their caves. The snow became deep, making it hard to walk.

One day a film of ice had formed over the lake. Amos broke the ice with a paw. He took a long drink of water. He shivered. He had never known water to be so cold.

He looked for fish along the water's edge. But there were none to be found.

He dug beneath the snow. Surely there would be roots. But the ground was not soft as in summer. He dug until he was almost ready to give up. But finally he had his dinner.

In a few days the ice on the lake was too thick to break. The ground was too hard to dig.

He ate some snow. Then he stood on his hind legs and sniffed the air. There was the faint odor of a farm nearby.

Quickly Amos was on his way. Just as he reached the barn, there was a loud *bang*. Amos didn't move from the corner of the barn. His heart quivered. He had heard sounds like that many times in the forest. He waited.

The sound came again and Amos chuckled. It was not the dreaded sound he had heard in the forest. It was a door to a corncrib that was banging in the wind. It was an invitation to dinner.

With a bound, Amos was inside the corncrib. He ignored the banging door as he devoured the corn.

Suddenly, there were voices. Amos leaped through the open door. Snow slid off the roof, nearly covering him. The voices grew louder.

With all his strength, Amos fought his way out of the snow. He fled to the forest. A man and a boy chased after him. Amos hid in thick underbrush. He sat very still. Soon the voices had turned back toward the farm.

Amos peeked around the brush. The wind had already covered their tracks. Slowly he trudged toward the cave. Mother and Father Bear would be waiting.

Snow had covered the entrance to the cave. Amos was so tired he could hardly lift a paw. But he dug and dug. Suddenly, a big hole opened up. Father Bear pushed through from the other side. "Now we can get some sleep," he said. "Have you learned enough?"

Amos hurried into the cave. He snuggled down beside Father and Mother Bear. Had he learned enough? Perhaps he had learned why bears sleep in the winter. Why did deer stay awake during the winter? Why did corn from a corncrib taste different than corn from a field? Why . . .

"Are you warm now, Amos?" Mother Bear asked. But the only answer was a gentle snore.

Little Wren's Gift

By Trinka Enell

In a far-off world that was ruled by animals, Little Wren landed lightly in an acacia tree outside the royal den. She flapped her wings in excitement. How proud the king and queen must be! After many years of waiting, the Queen of Beasts had at last given birth to a healthy male cub.

Fearsome Fish Hawk dropped from the sky and landed beside her, his yellow eyes flashing. He loomed over her. "And what are you giving the new prince for his birthday?" he demanded.

Little Wren wilted under that piercing gaze. "I am only a small wren," she stammered. "What could I offer the Prince of Beasts?"

"What indeed?" said Fish Hawk. "I've pledged to catch him a fresh fish every morning for his first year. But you," he snickered, "you are too small to catch anything but bugs!" Laughing, Fish Hawk soared away.

Little Wren hung her head. It was true. She was too little to catch even the smallest fish. But there must be something she could give the new prince. "I will ask Hippo," Little Wren decided. "She is wise in the ways of the world."

She found Hippo dozing in a deep pool in the Luwanga River. Only her nostrils and her twitching ears showed above the placid water. Little Wren landed on an ear and gave it a gentle peck. "Hippo!" she said. "Please come out. I need your help."

Water streaming off her rough gray skin, Hippo clambered up onto the riverbank. Her eyes gleamed with pleasure at the sight of Little Wren. "Little Wren, my small friend, how can I help?" she asked.

Little Wren fluttered her wings. "I want to give the new prince a gift to celebrate his birth," she told Hippo. "But the only thing I can catch are bugs and moths."

Hippo snorted laughter. "That is a problem," she agreed. "The king and queen would not be happy if you gave their son a gift of bugs!"

"Do you have a gift for the prince?" Little Wren asked. She rested on her friend's back.

Hippo nodded. "I have gathered a big bundle of ferns and rushes," she said. "They will make him a fine bed."

"Oh!" peeped Little Wren. "That is a lovely gift. But it would take me a month to gather enough ferns even for the new prince's head."

Hippo stretched out in the warm sand. "Every animal has its own strengths," she said. "I have big teeth that can clip swiftly through any amount of ferns." She chuckled. "And a bigger mouth to carry them in."

Little Wren had to laugh. It was true—Hippo had the biggest mouth she'd ever seen. Then Little Wren sighed. "I don't have any strengths," she said sadly.

Hippo snorted once more. "Nonsense! Every creature has a strength of one kind or another. Why don't you find a nice quiet place and think it over? If you think long enough, you're sure to come up with something."

"If I think that long, the prince will no longer be a cub!" Little Wren replied. But she thanked

Hippo for her advice and set out to find a quiet place to think.

An hour later Little Wren landed in the acacia tree beside the royal den. She couldn't find a quiet place anywhere else. Bellowing, chattering animals filled the forest and meadows, all intent on gathering presents for the little prince.

She closed her eyes and silence washed over her like a gentle breeze. Little Wren smiled. Of course—no animal would make noise here and chance disturbing the new prince. Now perhaps she'd be able to think of a gift for him.

Suddenly, a squalling roar filled the air. Little Wren's eyes snapped open. What in the world? The sound came again, louder and longer. "Oh!" peeped Little Wren, realizing the sound came from the royal cave. "It's the new prince. He must be very upset!"

The King of Beasts stumbled from the cave. His mane was uncombed and his eyes were tired.

"Is the prince sick?" Little Wren peeped anxiously.

The King of Beasts shook his head wearily. "He doesn't seem to be," he said. "He wakes up crying as if he's in pain. But we can find nothing wrong with him. Perhaps he's having nightmares, though he seems too young."

"Poor baby," said Little Wren. "I wish I could do something to help."

The king sighed heavily. "I, too," he said. "The queen is wearing herself out trying to soothe him."

Soothe him? All at once Little Wren smiled. Perhaps she did have a gift for the new prince! "With Your Majesty's permission," she said, "I would like to give my gift to your son now."

The king looked puzzled.

"My gift is the gift of song," Little Wren explained. "All wrens have possessed it from the dawn of time. It has been known to soothe even the most troubled creatures."

A smile enveloped the king's face. "That is a splendid gift!" he declared. "And a most welcome one."

Again the squalling roar filled the air. Quickly, Little Wren fluttered into the cave. "A splendid gift," she heard the King of Beasts repeat as he followed her inside. "The best gift a newborn cub could receive."

Joy bubbled up inside Little Wren like a flower bursting into bloom. Landing on a rocky spire near the prince's bed, she opened her beak and began to sing.

Barkley, Dog Detective

By Diana R. Jenkins

They call me Barkley. I don't know why. I don't bark. I can bark, but I don't. Not that much.

I'm a dogtective.

Dog + detective = dogtective.

I have a real nose for mysteries; solve most of them from this spot on the family-room rug.

Footsteps upstairs? Mr. Carter's in his den.

Strange smells? Tommy's been petting the bull-dog next door.

Mrs. Carter's trench coat missing? Kara wore it to school.

Grinding noises from the kitchen? Mr. Carter's making supper for yours truly.

Simple cases. Didn't have to move a whisker to solve them.

They're not all that easy. Sometimes a dogtective has to think. Sometimes he has to think hard. Sometimes he even has to move.

This is the story of one of those cases.

It was a Saturday afternoon like any other Saturday afternoon. I was at my usual post: the sunny spot on the family-room rug. Mr. Carter was on the couch, reading the paper. Tommy was hunting in the pantry for something to eat. Kara was cleaning her room. Mrs. Carter was putting on her coat to go shopping.

Everything seemed normal. Then Mrs. Carter drove off, and things began to happen.

Mr. Carter jumped up and ran through the kitchen to the garage. Tommy slammed the pantry door and dashed upstairs. Kara burst into the kitchen with a paper sack.

Sometimes a dogtective gets a feeling. I felt it. Something was happening. But what?

I decided to start with Tommy. I tracked him upstairs to his bedroom. He was on his bed, rustling paper. I stuck my nose over the edge, but before I saw anything, Tommy pushed me away and yelled, "Get your wet nose out of here, Barkley!" Then he pushed me out of the room and closed the door.

As if it's a crime to have a wet nose.

I headed downstairs. Mr. Carter was in the kitchen, holding a white box and looking for a place to put it. The box smelled delicious, so I was hoping he'd put it on the floor. No dice. He set it on the counter and said, "Now, if I can only find some matches."

Matches? Aha! A cookout. But where were the hot dogs? I sniffed around while Mr. Carter looked through the drawers. Just as he found some matches, a loud *pop!* came from the family room. I dashed off to investigate.

I found Kara sitting on the rug, surrounded by colorful balls. At least, they looked like balls. I poked one with my nose. It didn't feel like a ball. I picked one up in my mouth and quickly discovered the truth. It was a bomb, and it exploded right in my face!

"Barkley! Get out of here!" Kara shouted. She didn't have to tell me twice. I ran back to the kitchen and turned around, expecting to see her behind me. Instead, she was closing the family-room door.

She was closing herself in with the bombs!

Before I could do anything, Mr. Carter picked up the white box and the matches and took them into the family room, shutting the door behind him.

Then Tommy ran downstairs with a big box and went into the family room, too!

I had to warn them. I scratched at the door and whined, but they didn't understand.

"Can't Barkley come in?" asked Tommy.

"No!" said Kara.

I didn't want to come in. I wanted them to come out!

I waited outside that door a long time, wondering when the bombs would go off and thinking hard. Who made these clever bombs? Why were they in our family room? Where were the hot dogs?

I heard a sound that gave me hope. Mrs. Carter was driving into the garage. She would make them understand!

She came in with some sacks and put them on the kitchen table.

"Hello, Barkley," she said as she started taking things out of the sacks. Maybe she had the hot dogs.

I looked at the family-room door. She didn't notice. I whined.

"Just a minute, Barkley," she said. "There's a treat for you in here somewhere."

I barked. One short bark. Mrs. Carter looked at me in surprise. "Is something wrong, Barkley?" Then she noticed the closed door. "What's going on?"

When she opened the door, I hurried in to put myself between her and the bombs. I was surprised to see that the bombs were now hanging from the ceiling. Mr. Carter, Tommy, and Kara yelled, "Surprise!" as Mrs. Carter came into the room. Then they started singing.

A beautiful cake was sitting on the coffee table. The cake was on fire, but Mrs. Carter was never one to panic. She simply blew out the flames. Fortunately, the cake was unharmed, and she gave each of us a piece.

Then she ripped the paper from Tommy's box and took out a fluffy robe. "I love it!" she said. She kissed everyone and gave me more cake. Who needed hot dogs?

And the bombs? Well, even a dogtective can make a mistake. I must admit I felt foolish when I saw Tommy blow one up. I still don't understand why people want to save their air that way. I decided that mystery could wait for another day.

Sometimes a dogtective needs a nice, long nap in the sun.

The Most Welcome Guest

By Harriett Diller

Long ago in Shanghai the poorest families lived aboard riverboats of wood, tin, cloth, and straw patched together. Though they were very crowded, these families always found room for animals.

In just such a family Chicken lived. Every day she reminded herself how lucky she was to have a home in the straw under the bed. "As my good mother told me," she said, "everyone is not so fortunate."

Then one day a duck arrived.

Chicken watched as Duck strutted proudly across the straw and announced, "The dream of every floating hut-boat family is to own a duck."

Chicken was not at all sure she liked Duck's attitude or this change in her life. But she merely shrugged and said to herself, "As my good mother told me, always treat another as if she were the most welcome guest."

Life with Duck was not easy. She quacked. She strutted across the straw. But Chicken always treated her as if she were the most welcome guest.

A few weeks later Duck told Chicken she had a wonderful surprise. There in the straw were six eggs. Duck sat on them day after day. Soon they hatched into ducklings.

Chicken was not at all sure she liked this change. But she said to herself, "As my good mother told me, always treat another as if she were the most welcome guest. And I am sure she would have wanted me to treat another's children as if they were the most welcome guests, too."

Life with Duck and her six ducklings was not easy. Soon Duck lost all her old feathers and grew new ones. The cozy home under the bed became a blizzard of duck feathers. The ducklings quacked even more than their mother. The whole duck family strutted proudly across the straw. But Chicken always treated them as if they were the most welcome guests.

Weeks passed. One day a young pig arrived. Pig took up so much space that Chicken, Duck, and the ducklings had to crowd into the dark corner at the back of the straw.

Chicken was not at all sure she liked this change. But she shrugged and said to herself, "As my good mother told me, always treat another as if he were the most welcome guest."

Life with Pig was the hardest yet. He snorted and grunted and snored. He was a messy eater who slopped his food from one end of the straw to the other. But Chicken always treated Pig as if he were the most welcome guest.

One summer morning Duck whispered to Chicken, "I have a plan. Pig likes two things, eating and sleeping. But what if we eat his food while he sleeps? Then Pig will be unhappy and leave our floating hut-boat."

It was a terribly hot day. And if it is hot in Shanghai, it is even hotter inside a tiny floating hut-boat with a tin roof. And hotter still under the bed of a floating hut-boat. And hottest of all if you must share that space with one duck, six almost-grown ducklings, and an ever-expanding pig.

Such conditions seemed to excuse bad manners.

"All right," Chicken said to Duck. "I'll help you."

But when the food came, Chicken couldn't go through with the plan. "This food belongs to Pig, not us," she said.

Duck and the six ducklings began to gobble down the food scraps the family had shoved under the bed for Pig.

After a few bites Duck stopped eating. "You are right," she said.

Chicken nodded. "As my good mother told me, never take what belongs to another."

Duck groaned. "As my good mother told me, never eat pig food."

Duck and the six ducklings never stopped trying to drive Pig away. They quacked and snapped and flapped their wings. They complained about Pig's snorting and grunting and snoring. There was never a moment's peace under the bed of the floating hut-boat.

Summer ended. The days grew short. Shanghai is cold in winter and a floating hut-boat even colder, for poor families have no money to buy coal.

"I don't know which is worse," Duck said one bitter night when wind rattled the tin roof and Pig's snores shook the floor, "winter or Pig."

Chicken shivered. "As my good mother told me, the wise bird flies south for the winter."

"Oh, you and your good mother," Duck snapped.

Pig snorted once, grunted twice, and snored three times.

"Quiet!" Duck flapped her wings at Pig.

"Let him sleep," said Chicken. "I'd sleep if I weren't so cold."

Pig snorted, grunted, and snored all over again. Then he rolled toward Chicken and Duck and her family of now-grown children.

"This is too much!" Duck cried. "Let's make him think twice about sprawling into our corner."

Duck's children quacked in agreement.

Chicken shook her head. "Why start a fight?"

Minutes passed. Still, Pig crowded Chicken and the seven ducks into the corner. *I don't know how much longer I can keep the others from fighting Pig,* thought Chicken. The cold was bad enough, but she hated fighting even more. Chicken was just about to wake Pig and ask him as politely as possible to move when she noticed a new feeling.

"It's been so long I'm not quite sure, but I think I'm warm. And it's much too early for spring."

Now Chicken realized where the warmth was coming from. "Move over here next to me, Duck," she said. "Bring your children." She snuggled even closer to Pig.

"No need to fly south for the winter," Chicken said. "If we stay together like this, we'll be warm."

All that long winter the animals under the bed of the floating hut-boat stayed close and warm. Of course, Duck and her family continued to quack. Of course, Pig continued to snort and grunt and slop food. But Chicken did her best to ignore their shortcomings. For they *were* the most welcome guests.

Sausage Heaven

By Marianne Mitchell

Snug inside his mousehole, Ratón Pepe twitched his whiskery nose. He slowly uncurled his long tail. Why was waking up so hard today? He wiggled his nose again, searching for those yummy breakfast smells. He opened one eye to see if he was still in his own home. Yes, this was the place. Sausage Heaven, the best restaurant in Seville, Spain. But where were the usual smells of fresh coffee, baking bread, and spicy meats?

"Something's wrong," said Pepe, jumping out of bed. "I'd better find Mr. Acosta."

He patted his fur and poked his head out of his mousehole. Loud voices drifted down the hall. Pepe scurried off to the kitchen to investigate.

In the kitchen, the rickety smoker-oven stood silent and cold. A jumble of grinders, mixers, and stuffers stuck out in all directions. For a hundred years the smoker-oven had cranked out the best sausages in town.

Pepe hopped over the oily rags and tools on the floor and ducked behind a string of garlic. A big, sooty workman scooted out from behind the oven.

"I'm sorry, Mr. Acosta. This old oven is a wreck. A new one is your only hope," the workman said as he wiped a greasy rag across his face.

"But this oven is one-of-a-kind," said Mr. Acosta. "I can't just go out and buy another one!"

"I might be able to fix it, but it would cost a lot of money." The workman gathered up his tools and went out the door.

Pepe watched a big tear roll down Mr. Acosta's cheek. He ran over to him, squeaking words of sympathy. Mr. Acosta's big hands reached down and picked him up.

"Now what will I do, my little friend? I don't have a lot of money. We may soon be out of a home."

Pepe jumped down and ran back to his warm bed. He buried his head under the covers. *Maybe this is just a bad dream,* thought Pepe.

But it wasn't a dream. He had to find a way to help his old friend. Unlike most restaurant owners, Mr. Acosta liked having a mouse around. Pepe always cleaned the floor of crumbs, grapes, cheese, or bits of sausages that fell from the tables. Even the customers laughed as Pepe ran from table to table, munching on scraps.

Sometimes Pepe found things he couldn't eat. He dragged them home and shoved them under his straw bed. Pepe hopped down and peered under his bed. "Let's see if I have something that will help," said Pepe. He pulled out six keys, nine hairpins, one comb, five bottle caps, seven buttons, four pens, and two coins. Only two coins. He needed a million coins. But maybe he had the tools to fix the oven.

Out the mousehole and down the hall, Pepe lugged his blanket full of little treasures. Mr. Acosta still sat like a lump in the kitchen, staring at his broken oven.

Pepe dragged his blanket under the oven and went to work with his "tools." He wiggled hairpins in the cracks. He poked keys into any slot big enough. Why didn't the old oven zoom to life like a race car? He jammed a bottle cap or a button next to any loose or rattling parts. The pens became substitute levers. The comb went under a wobbly leg. Nothing worked.

All he had left were the two coins. Pepe knew that people used them to pay for things. "Bah! Two coins aren't enough," said Pepe. He gave his blanket a shake. The coins rolled across the floor to Mr. Acosta's feet.

"What have you found, Pepe?" said Mr. Acosta, picking them up. "Ha! One shiny peseta! But what's this?" He looked at the second one for a long time. "I've never seen a coin like this before. Come on, my friend," said Mr. Acosta. "Let's see what we can find out." He picked up Pepe, slipped him into his shirt pocket with the coin, and walked out the door.

When Pepe finally peeked out, he saw they were on a small street lined with busy shops. Mr. Acosta went into a little shop crammed full of books and boxes. Pepe liked this place. It reminded him of his cluttered mousehole.

"What kind of coin is this?" Mr. Acosta asked the man behind the counter.

The man took out a magnifying glass and studied the coin. Next, he looked in a huge, worn book. He looked at the coin again.

"Where did you find this?" asked the man. "It's more than five hundred years old. It dates back to the time of King Ferdinand and Queen Isabella."

"But is it worth anything?" asked Mr. Acosta.

"In the old days it was worth twenty excelentes."

"I need pesetas, not excelentes. Are you saying this coin is worthless?"

"No, sir! According to my book, it's worth about a million pesetas," said the man.

"A million pesetas! For one coin?" Mr. Acosta gasped. "Hooray! We're saved, Pepe!"

A few days later, snug inside his mousehole, Ratón Pepe woke to delicious smells. His nose twitched, his tail uncurled, and he opened both eyes at once. Mmmm! He smelled fresh coffee, baking bread, and spicy sausages. At last the newly fixed smoker-oven was hard at work cranking out delicious sausages. Pepe would have many more happy years in Sausage Heaven.

This is a made-up story. But if you travel someday to Seville, Spain, go to the restaurant Hosteria del Laurel in the Santa Cruz neighborhood. There you will see the sealed-up mousehole where the real Ratón Pepe once lived.

Clara Crumpet Cleans Up

By Heather Dancer

Clara Crumpet, the badger, opened her closet door. *Buffle! Kafuffle! Bangitty-Bop!*

Out tumbled a terrible tangle of roller skates, gloves, galoshes, fourteen umbrellas, and an orange straw hat trimmed with purple fringe.

"Why, bless my badger bristles!" exclaimed Clara. "I had better clean this closet."

When she was done, the closet was as clean as new clothes, but three umbrellas, a roller skate, and the straw hat were left over.

I'll put them away in the attic, thought Clara. She got her ladder and climbed up, pushing open the trapdoor to the attic. *Swoosh! Ploosh! Floppity-Ploppity-Plop!* Down came five mattresses, six puzzles (each missing one piece), twenty-nine Halloween masks, and two broken lamps.

Clara clung to the ladder. "Upon my grandmother's nose," she said breathlessly. "The attic needs cleaning more than the closet did."

She set to work. Soon the attic was shining like the sun, but a mattress, two puzzles, seventeen masks, and the straw hat were left over.

Clara looked at them, dusting off her hands. "These will keep nicely in the basement, I think," she said happily.

She lugged them downstairs and opened the basement door. *Sproing! Boing! Clackitty-Clatter!* Pogo sticks, folding chairs, bricks, brackets, and odd knickknacks leaped out all around her.

"I'll be an ant's anklebone," cried Clara. "I had no idea the basement was such a mess."

Two hours later Clara was dusty and covered with cobwebs, but the basement sparkled like diamonds. Only a pogo stick, seven folding chairs, ninety-two bricks, and the straw hat were left over.

"To the garage with you," said Clara, gathering an armload of bricks.

She lifted the garage door. *Clang! Bang! Rackitty-Splatter!* Out burst three dented garbage cans, twelve rusty rakes, and two leaky hoses.

"Well, good gracious," Clara gasped. "The garage is the worst yet!"

She scrubbed and tidied until the garage was as neat as a noodle.

An enormous pile of leftover objects sat in the driveway, with the straw hat on top. Just then Marvin Muskrat tapped Clara on the shoulder. "Pardon me. Are you having a garage sale?"

What a good idea, thought Clara. "Yes, I am," she said. People flocked in, and soon everything was sold. (Even the straw hat. Clara bought it herself.)

After everyone had left, Clara pulled out her wallet to put away the money from the garage sale. Out of her pocket popped cough drops, a comb, tissues, keys, coins, notepaper, and pencils.

She put on her straw hat and walked to the store. She bought a pair of pants with eight pockets—one for cough drops, one for her comb, one for tissues, one for keys, one for coins, one for notepaper, one for pencils, and one for her wallet.

With her new pants on and all the pockets organized, Clara sat down. "I think I'll take a little nap," she said with a yawn. "Then I'll clean out the kitchen cupboards."

A Visit
from
Cousin
Eddie

By Marty Rhodes Figley

Knock! Knock! Knock! Arthur opened his door. A large elephant in a loud blue shirt was standing there.

"Hello, Arthur, I'm your Cousin Eddie. I've come to spend the day."

"Oh, my." Arthur hardly knew what to say. He hadn't seen Cousin Eddie for years.

Cousin Eddie stepped in. "I thought you might show me the sights."

Arthur stammered, "W-well, we could go to my club for lunch and then maybe take a walk on the beach."

"Splendid!" Cousin Eddie tried to help Arthur with his coat. He tugged as Arthur pulled. *R-r-i-p!*

"Oh, my." Arthur hardly knew what to say. His favorite brown tweed jacket with the patch pockets had a big tear in the back.

"Why, what good fortune!" Cousin Eddie exclaimed. "If you overindulge at lunch and your waistline expands, your coat won't be too tight."

The two elephants took a taxi to the club. The headwaiter seated them at a table by the window. When the food was served, Arthur dipped his spoon into his vegetable soup and pulled out a cockroach.

"Oh, my." Arthur hardly knew what to say.

Cousin Eddie stood up and waved his arms. "Waiter! You forgot the cockroach for my soup!" He smiled at Arthur. "What a good idea. There is so much protein in cockroaches."

Arthur urged his cousin to sit down and gallantly offered Eddie his soup with the cockroach included.

After lunch they took a walk on the beach. Cousin Eddie said, "Let's build a sand castle. We had better remove our shoes so the sand won't get in them."

The two cousins worked for an hour constructing an enormous sand castle with many turrets. As they finished the moat, Cousin Eddie said, "We seem to have lost our shoes."

"Oh, my." Arthur hardly knew what to say. Those were the brand-new brown loafers he had purchased at one of the finer department stores.

Cousin Eddie smiled. "Well, if we don't find them we can walk barefoot on the beach and feel the sand between our toes."

Nevertheless, the elephants dug up the sand castle, hoping to find the shoes. Sand flew everywhere. Some of it hit the Horrible Hippo Brothers, who were sunbathing nearby.

Hud Hippo jumped up and snarled. "What do you think you're doing, kicking sand in my face? My brother and I will show you a thing or two!"

"Oh, my." Arthur hardly knew what to say. But suddenly he and Cousin Eddie were running barefoot on the beach with the two Horrible Hippo Brothers close behind.

Cousin Eddie was breathing hard. "This is superb exercise. If they don't catch us, we will certainly feel healthier after our run."

Finally Arthur and Eddie were able to duck behind a hot dog stand, and the Horrible Hippo Brothers ran by.

The tired elephants hailed a taxi.

Back at the apartment they lounged on Arthur's living-room sofa, sipping lemonade. Cousin Eddie sighed and stood up. "Well, Arthur, I guess it's time for me to go," he said. The two cousins shook hands.

At the door Cousin Eddie paused and smiled at Arthur. "Perhaps I'll come to see you next year."

"Oh, my." Arthur thought of his torn coat, the cockroach, the lost shoes, and the Horrible Hippo Brothers. It had been one of the most exciting, wonderful days he could remember.

Arthur knew exactly what to say.

"Yes, next year would be splendid."

Bears
Are
Scary

By Bonnie Highsmith Taylor

Every morning before Buster Bear went out to play, his father and mother would tell him:

"Bears are scary, bears are scary.
Bears are big and black and hairy.
Bears say OOO! And bears say WOO!
Bears are big and scary."

But Buster wasn't scary. Not one little bit. He couldn't even scare Midji Mouse, who was afraid of her own shadow.

It was true that he was black and hairy, but he certainly wasn't very big.

"You will be someday, though," Father Bear explained. "And you must learn how to be fierce and scary. To be the ruler of the forest."

Buster didn't want to be fierce and scary. He didn't care about being the ruler of the forest. Buster loved all the little animals and wanted to be friends with them.

But he knew his mother and father were disappointed in him, so he tried. He really tried very hard each day.

As he walked through the forest, Buster practiced howling and scowling and growling and hunching and scrunching.

"Bears are scary!" he roared. *"Bears are scary!*
Bears are big and black and hairy.
Bears say OOO! And bears say WOO!
Bears are big and scary."

After a while he spied Rondi Rabbit beside the trail, nibbling in a patch of sweet clover.

"I'll scare the wits right out of him," Buster said aloud. "I'll show him who rules the forest."

Buster said, "OOO!" He said, "WOO!" He grumbled and rumbled and howled and growled.

But Rondi didn't twitch an ear or a whisker. He just said, without looking up from the sweet clover he was nibbling, "What's the matter, Buster? Got a tummyache?"

"Aw," sighed Buster. "Isn't anyone afraid of me?"

But he wouldn't give up. He kept on trying to be fierce. He had to please his mother and father.

On and on he went until he came upon Chester Chipmunk taking a nap on a log.

"I'll scare the wits right out of him," Buster said aloud. "I'll show him who rules the forest!"

Buster said, "OOO!" He said, "WOO!" He grumbled and rumbled and howled and growled.

All Chester said was, "My gosh, Buster, keep quiet. Can't a fellow take a nap around here?"

Buster shrugged his shoulders and slowly walked away. It wasn't easy trying to please Mother and Father Bear. He didn't look fierce. He didn't act fierce. But most of all, he didn't feel fierce.

He knew he had to keep trying. Someday he would be a grown-up bear. And who ever heard of a grown-up bear that no one was scared of?

When Buster got to the river he saw Dori Deer daintily drinking water. Dori was very shy.

"I'll scare the wits right out of her," Buster said aloud. "I'll show her who's master of the forest."

Buster said, "OOO!" He said, "WOO!" He grumbled and rumbled and howled and growled.

And did he scare Dori out of her wits? No. Did he frighten her even a teeny weeny bit? No. Dori turned around and stamped her foot sharply. "For shame, Buster," she said. "Have you no manners? Excuse yourself at once."

Buster meekly excused himself and hurried on his way.

But he kept on practicing being fierce. He grumbled at Fiona Frog. Fiona smiled. He rumbled at Sonny Skunk. Sonny giggled. He howled at Wendy Woodchuck. Wendy snickered. And he growled at Ozzie Owl. Ozzie chuckled.

Buster practiced so hard that by the time he got home he had lost his voice completely.

"Whatever is the matter?" asked his mother.

"I—I can't talk," Buster whispered hoarsely.

"Laryngitis," said Father Bear. "I get it myself at times when I've been unusually fierce."

"I know just the thing for that," Mother Bear exclaimed. She took a bottle from a shelf on the wall. "My own special remedy," she said.

It looked awful. It smelled terrible. It tasted horrible. Buster shuttered and sputtered. He gulped and he gasped.

Then out the door and off through the forest he ran, first on two legs, then on all four. "OOO! OOO!" he moaned loudly. "WOO! WOO!" he groaned. He rumbled and grumbled and howled and growled.

"Look out!" shouted Midji Mouse. "It's a bear! A big, hairy, scary bear!"

The animals scampered in all directions. Down a hole went Rondi Rabbit. Up a tree went Chester Chipmunk. Through the bushes went Dori Deer.

When the bad taste was gone and the burning had stopped, Buster realized what had happened. He had scared all the animals out of their wits.

Most of the time Buster is still his usual good-natured self. But every now and then, when he feels the need to be masterful, he lumbers through the forest shouting:

"Bears are scary, bears are scary.
Bears are big and black and hairy.
Bears say OOO! And bears say WOO!
Bears are big and scary."

And all the other animals agree.

Outfoxing the Fox

By Nancy Lemke

Arnold was an old farm dog. He'd served the farmer well for many years, and now he was enjoying himself, eating steak every Saturday evening and taking long naps in front of the fire.

But one day the farmer startled Arnold.

"Arnold, you spend so much time sleeping that I don't think you can keep the hens safe from the fox anymore. If you don't perk up, I'm going to have to get a new watchdog."

Oh no! thought Arnold. He didn't want to lose his job. So he went to see the fox.

He told the fox his problem. "Can you help me?" he asked.

"Sure," said the fox. "Tonight I'll pretend to break into the hen house. You bark loud enough to wake the farmer. When he catches sight of us, I'll run off. He'll think you're the greatest watchdog that ever lived."

Arnold trotted home happily, thinking of steaks and the warm hearth by the fire.

That night everything went as the fox predicted.

"I was wrong about you," said the farmer after he'd seen Arnold chase the fox. "You're a great watchdog. You can stay here forever."

"Oh, boy," sighed Arnold. And he curled up happily on the farmer's hearth.

The next night, however, the fox returned.

"You're supposed to be gone," said Arnold.

"I changed my mind," said the fox. "Bring me three fat hens tomorrow night, or I'll show the farmer you didn't get rid of me at all."

Arnold was worried again. "OK," he agreed. "I'll bring them."

Arnold spent a sleepless night, wondering what to do. Finally, he had an idea. The next day he took three hens to the fox's den.

"I brought the hens," he told the fox. "But I have to warn you: These aren't eating hens; they're working hens. Each one has a special skill that helps around the farm. They pass this skill to their chicks and to anyone who eats them. If I were you, I wouldn't touch them."

"Hogwash!" said the fox. "Hens are hens. Send them in here."

The first hen stumbled in wearing enormous red shoes.

"Why are you wearing those shoes?" asked the fox, staring at the two crimson clodhoppers.

"To cover my feet," said the hen.

"But those shoes are gigantic," said the fox.

"So are my feet," said the hen. "My big feet are great for threshing wheat."

"What are your chicks like?" asked the fox.

"They stumble all over," the hen said proudly.

The fox looked at his own dainty paws. Every evening as the sun set, the fox loved to dance and skip through the meadows. If his feet grew huge after eating this hen, he'd only thump and bump.

"Send in the next hen," he said.

A moment later the second hen walked in and collapsed on the floor.

"The poor thing," said the fox. "She fainted from fright."

"Oh no," said the hen. "This is my job."

"Your job?" asked the fox.

"Oh yes," said the hen. "Being limp is my job. The farmer uses me to dust. The limper I am, the tinier the cracks I can reach."

"But you walked in here all right," said the fox.

"Well, sometimes I can walk," said the hen, "but mostly I'm limp."

"What are your chicks like?" asked the fox.

"Floppy all over," said the hen.

The fox was so hungry that his stomach hurt, but he knew he couldn't eat this hen.

"What's the last hen like?" he asked Arnold.

"Huge teeth," Arnold answered. "She chops down trees in seconds."

The fox's eyes lit up. "Dinner is finally served," he said. "Send her in."

The last hen walked in, grinning. Huge teeth gleamed from her beak.

The fox put on his bib and set the hen on his lap. He was just about to sprinkle her with salt when she said, "Mr. Fox, after I'm gone, please tell my little toothless ones I said good-bye."

"Toothless ones?" asked the fox.

"My chicks," said the hen.

"Your chicks?" said the fox. "But your chicks are supposed to have huge teeth just like yours."

"I know," said the hen. "But it seems to work backward with me. Who knows what will happen to whoever eats me."

The fox thought about this, but not for long. He threw off his bib, shoved the hen off his lap, and ran out the door. He was never seen again.

Peace returned to the farm. The hens lived safely in their hen house, and Arnold had steak every Saturday night.

The people, however, had new problems. The farmer's wife couldn't find her dancing shoes. And the farmer's false teeth never did turn up, either.

A **Day** for **Adventure**

By Diane Taylor

"Come on in, Gordie. The water's great!" Louis Raccoon paddled from one side of the pond to the other. He did the backstroke. He did the dog paddle. He even did somersaults. He was having a wonderful time.

His friend Gordon Turtle stood on the bank with his head pulled back in his shell.

Louis got out of the water and shook his wet fur. "Ah, that was wonderful. What should we do next?"

"Sit and watch the leaves change colors?" Gordon asked.

"Sit! Too tame for us today, Gordie my pal. This day was meant for adventure!" Louis leaned back on his friend's shell and thought. "Now, let's see . . . Hey, I've got it!" he shouted. "Let's have a race to that big tree over there."

Louis crouched in his sprinting position and said, "Ready. Set. GO!" He shot off as if he'd been hurled from a slingshot. Back at the edge of the pond sat Gordon. He hadn't taken one step.

Louis cartwheeled over to Gordon. "Hey, Gordie, not feeling well today? House payments getting you down?" Louis slapped the turtle's shell and burst out laughing at his joke. "House payments. Get it?"

Gordon didn't laugh. He didn't smile. He didn't even look at Louis. He trembled slightly and his long neck drooped out of his shell as he stared at the ground.

"Hey, ol' buddy, it was only a joke," Louis apologized. "Don't look so downhearted."

"It's not your fault, Louis. It's just that . . . " Gordon hesitated, then let out a big sigh. "I'm embarrassed to tell you."

Louis put a paw around Gordon's neck. "Aw, come on, Gordie. We're best friends. You can tell me anything."

Without taking his eyes off the ground Gordon said, "I'm afraid."

"Afraid!" Louis yelled. Then, too shocked to say anything else, he yelled it again. "Afraid?"

"Would you please stop saying . . . that word?"

"I'm sorry, Gordie."

The turtle's little head was practically dragging on the ground. "I know what you're thinking. Go ahead and say it. I'm a chicken turtle."

"Don't talk like that," Louis snapped. "A chicken is a bird. A turtle is a reptile. The two have absolutely nothing in common—except soup." Louis chuckled and swatted his friend's back. "Soup. Get it? Chicken soup? Turtle soup?"

Gordon lifted his teary eyes and said, "This isn't a laughing matter."

Louis sat on Gordon's shell and asked, "OK, buddy, tell ol' Louis—what is it that you're afraid of?"

Gordon thought for a few seconds, then said in an even sadder voice, "I don't know. I'm just afraid!"

"I think I understand," Louis said. "I was afraid once myself."

Gordon couldn't believe his little turtle ears. "You? What on earth were you afraid of?"

Louis jumped off his friend's back, looked him square in the eyes, then said in a whisper, "Of the dark."

"The dark?" Gordon said. "But raccoons are nocturnal animals. Doesn't that mean you enjoy doing things at night? Hunting. Climbing trees. Moon bathing."

"Hold on," Louis interrupted. "I've never been one for moon bathing. But I'm telling you, the first time my father sent me crayfish hunting at night, I nearly shivered my stripes off, I shook so hard with fear."

"How did you get over it?" Gordon asked.

"First, I asked myself exactly what it was about the dark that frightened me."

"What was your answer?" Gordon asked.

Louis let his eyes wander across the vastness of their forest home and said, "I didn't know what was out there."

Gordon looked confused. "But didn't you know the only thing that changed was the light? Everything else stayed the same."

"It took me awhile, but I finally figured it out." Louis draped an arm around his friend's wrinkled neck. "So, Gordie my pal, just ask yourself what exactly is scaring you. Then you can start to solve your problem."

Gordon thought hard for a few moments, then said, "I think I'm afraid that I'm going to goof up and everyone will laugh at me."

"Goof up?" Louis jumped up and waved his arms in the air. "Goof up? Gordie, everyone's middle name should be 'Goof Up.' We all goof up. It's just part of being alive. The only way to learn is to take chances. And when we take chances, we're bound to goof up at times. But it's OK. Don't you remember how Mockingbird used to sit for hours practicing his calls? He certainly goofed up more high notes than a centipede has legs. And what about Rabbit? Does she give up running just because she loses a race now and then?"

"I see what you mean," Gordon said, a smile creeping across his thin turtle lips.

"Besides," Louis continued, "I'm your friend. I'd never make fun of you."

Gordon was beginning to feel like a new turtle. He swung his long neck out of his shell and took a deep breath of the fresh forest air. "It's time for me to start taking a few chances, 'sticking my neck out' as they say." Gordon nudged his friend and snickered. "A turtle sticking his neck out. Get it?"

The two friends looked at each other and burst out laughing. They laughed so hard their voices bounced from tree to tree until the echoes faded into the clearing at the end of the forest.

"How about that swim?" Gordon asked his raccoon friend.

"Sounds great to me," replied Louis.

Then arm in arm they made their way down to the pond. This was indeed a day for adventure.

The Tippytoes Have a Party

By Virginia Hackney

Once there was a family of mice that lived in a beautiful castle. The mice answered to the names of Papa Tippytoe, Mama Tippytoe, and little Martha Tippytoe.

In the evenings, they strolled hand in hand, looking at the flowered walls, the silk curtains, and the shiny floors made of marble. Sometimes Martha Tippytoe would see herself as she darted past the brass jars on the floor. She would sing *"Squeak, squeak, squeak!"* Mama Tippytoe would always say, "Now, Martha, we are uninvited guests in this part of the castle, and we must be very quiet." Then they would tiptoe to the back of the castle to their own little place—not wanting to wake Lady Samona.

In the middle of the castle stood two huge doors. Martha and her family had never seen what was behind them. Every day Martha would sit by the doors, cupping her ear as close as she dared, hoping to learn more about what was behind the sealed entrance.

One day Martha watched Alto, one of the servants, carrying large trays over his head. The door opened just a crack. Martha Tippytoe heard Lady Samona say to Alto, "When the clock strikes four, bring me my blue ruffled robe. And when the clock strikes five, bring me my gold cane. And at the stroke of six, unlock the doors and let my guests come in."

Martha Tippytoe rushed excitedly to her home. She said to Papa and Mama Tippytoe, "May we please be at the doors when the clock strikes six? Alto is going to unlock them." Mama and Papa Tippytoe nodded their heads.

Mama Tippytoe worked hard making their robes for the evening. She finished Papa Tippytoe's gray robe as the clock struck four. She slipped on her new pink robe as the clock struck five. By the time the clock struck six, Martha was dressed in her new red robe.

Through the doors came tall people, short people, fat people, skinny people, young people, and old people dressed in their finest clothes. At the end of the line, the mouse family tiptoed in. No one seemed to notice the uninvited guests.

Martha gazed at the food. Tables of cheeses—cheddar, blue, mozzarella, and Swiss—and tables of fruit—oranges, apples, bananas, and grapes—were arranged in the center of the room. Platters of meat and the music that flowed through the room made Martha spin with delight.

The people laughed, and the mouse family laughed. The people danced, and Mama and Papa Tippytoe danced. Martha sat and nibbled on a piece of cheddar.

Time passed, and Martha heard Lady Samona say, "What a fine party this is," and someone else added, "What a lovely room for a party." Martha's ears perked up. *So this is a party*, she thought. Papa Tippytoe had once read her a story about a party, but she had never been to one.

The clock in the hallway struck twelve. Lady Samona announced that the party was over and that they would be closing the doors soon.

Martha looked for Papa and Mama Tippytoe. She stumbled over Lady Samona's feet. Martha sang, *"Squeak, squeak, squeak!"*

Lady Samona screamed, "Eek, eek, eek!"

Out the doors ran the tall people, short people, fat people, skinny people, young people, and old people. Mama and Papa and Martha ran out, not making a sound.

Martha still tiptoes around the castle, but she never asks to go back to the party room. Now, when the clock strikes six, the Tippytoes open their doors and let their friends come in. There are fat mice, skinny mice, tall mice, short mice, young mice, and old mice.

The Tippytoe family laughs, and their friends laugh. The Tippytoe family dances, and their friends dance. Martha nibbles on a piece of cheddar.

And what a fine party all the mice have behind their own little doors.

No Ordinary Pig

By Lloydene L. Cook

Alexander held his head high and strutted around the pigpen. *What a special pig I am,* he thought. *There is no one else quite like me.*

While the other pigs wallowed in the squishy mud, Alexander strolled through Mrs. Green's rose garden sniffing the blossoms.

When the other pigs pushed and shoved and gobbled the food in their trough, Alexander nibbled on rutabagas in the vegetable garden. He didn't really like the taste, but they looked so special.

But no matter how special Alexander tried to be, the other animals seemed not to notice or care. *It's lonely being special,* thought Alexander.

One day Alexander discovered a large trunk. Curious, he lifted the lid. Inside he found a pair of striped trousers, a checkered jacket, a white shirt, a gold silk vest, and a polka-dot necktie. He also found a pair of high-top shoes, a straw hat, and a shiny red walking stick.

"Now the other animals have to notice how special I am," said Alexander.

Alexander put on the clothes and pranced down the lane. As he passed by the pond, he twirled around and admired his reflection in the water.

As soon as he reached the barnyard, Alexander puffed out his chest and pointed his nose in the air. He tipped his straw hat to the animals he passed.

"Hee haw," laughed the donkey. "Look at him—Mr. Fancy Pants!"

"Cluck, cluck," said the hen. "Who does he think he is?"

"How silly," snorted one of the pigs.

Alexander hurried past them. *They're just jealous,* he thought.

The sun sizzled overhead. Alexander loosened his tie. His jacket made him much too warm, so he took it off.

Alexander strolled into the rose garden and bent down to sniff a rosebud. He snagged his silk vest on some thorns.

In the vegetable garden, Alexander took a bite of rutabaga. A parade of ants crawled inside the sleeve of his shirt and bit him. "Ouch!" he squealed and wiggled out of the shirt.

A gust of wind sent his straw hat sailing into the air. "Come back," he cried. He tried to run after it, but the high-top shoes were too heavy.

Alexander kicked one shoe into the air, then the other one. "I don't need these pants, either," he said, taking them off. "I'm not a gentleman. I'm just an ordinary pig."

Sadly, Alexander sneaked back into his pen. The other pigs were too busy eating to notice him. Alexander walked over and sniffed at what they were eating. He took a small bite. "Hmm, not bad."

Next, Alexander wandered over to the mud-hole where some pigs were happily splashing and rolling about. "Come on in, Alexander," one pig called.

Alexander stuck in one hoof. The cool, slippery mud oozed between his toes. He put in the other hoof. Then he lay down and rolled around. He played in the mud with the other pigs for a long time.

When the sun dropped low in the sky, Alexander sighed and snuggled deeper in the mud. The other pigs were already asleep. For the very first time, Alexander understood what it meant to be a pig.

He didn't have to wear fancy clothes or eat rutabagas. He could roll in the mud and eat from the trough. He could be an ordinary pig and still be special.

"There is no one else quite like me," Alexander sighed. Then, beneath the round, silvery moon, he fell asleep.

Chelsea,
the
Fraidycat

By Dorothy Baughman

Chelsea lay on her stomach on the porch of Granny Martin's house. She crossed her paws and pretended to sleep. She could hear the other black cats discussing Halloween, but she tried not to listen.

"I wish the other cats would not expect me to go out on Halloween," Chelsea muttered. "Screeching and scaring people is not for me."

"Chelsea, the old fraidycat!" called the leader.

"Ha, ha," laughed the other cats. "Chelsea is too afraid to go out tonight."

One of the cats slipped quietly behind Chelsea. "Boo!" he yelled loudly.

"Meoweee!" cried Chelsea. Her fur stood up, and she jumped straight up into the air.

"Ha, ha, ha!" The other cats rolled on the ground in gleeful laughter.

Poor Chelsea. She slunk into the house, and crawled into her bed. "I'll just stay here until Halloween is over."

The skies were beginning to darken, and Chelsea's tummy began to rumble. She was hungry. She went into the well-lit kitchen and meowed around Granny Martin's legs to let her know she wanted her dinner.

"Scat, Chelsea! Get out of my way! I have to bake some cookies for the children when they come to trick or treat."

Chelsea scurried out of her way. "Humph," she sniffed. "Even Granny is celebrating Halloween."

It was getting darker and darker outside. Chelsea peeked out the window. Little goblins, witches, and ghosts were beginning to make their rounds. She heard the cats tuning up. *Meowooo, meowooo, meowoo.*

Chelsea shuddered. "I'm glad I'm not out there." Even though Chelsea didn't like Halloween, she would have made a good Halloween cat. Her fur was black and sleek, and she had enormous green eyes.

"Oh, fiddle-faddle, I'm really hungry now," she said. Back to the kitchen she went, but Granny was not there. Chelsea sniffed. The baking cookies made her mouth water. Three batches were stacked on the table.

"Maybe I could sneak just one cookie before she gets back." Chelsea raised herself up on her back legs. She could just reach the top of the table. She took a swipe with one paw and accidently hit Granny's flour sack.

Plop! The flour hit Chelsea right on the head. Flour flew everywhere, even in Chelsea's eyes.

It scared her so badly that she ran out the door, meowing at the top of her lungs. She ran on into the street, right through the group of black cats that was making plans to go Halloweening.

"Yeow, what in the world was that?" cried the leader. "It looked like a ghost cat!" All the cats meowed loudly and ran away from Chelsea as fast as they could.

By this time, Chelsea had wiped most of the flour out of her eyes. *What is the matter with those cats?* she thought.

Chelsea looked down at herself. "No wonder," she said and laughed. "I have flour all over me."

Chelsea made quite a sight. She had flour from the top of her ears to the tip of her tail. No one would have ever known she was really a black cat.

"They thought I was a ghost!" Chelsea exclaimed with glee.

The next morning, all the cats talked about was the horrible-looking cat that had scared them so badly.

"Boy, Chelsea," said one. "If you had seen that thing, you would have been scared out of your wits. It sure looked spooky."

Chelsea just smiled to herself and finished washing her whiskers.

From now on she was going to celebrate Halloween every year. And she knew just how she would do it.

Wallpaper!

By Eric A. Kimmel

Mr. Beetle sat in his living room listening to the radio. Happy music was playing, but Mr. Beetle didn't feel happy. "I feel sad," he said.

"Are you sad? Does everything make you blue?" the radio was saying.

"Yes," said Mr. Beetle.

"Then the answer for you is . . . WALLPAPER! Brighten you dingy den with a peppy pattern today. Let wallpaper put a smile back in your life."

"The radio is right," said Mr. Beetle. "I need new wallpaper. I'm going to buy some."

Mr. Beetle drove to the wallpaper store. He went inside. There were so many pretty patterns. Mr. Beetle couldn't make up his mind.

"May I help you?" the clerk said.

"I want to buy some wallpaper," said Mr. Beetle. "I also have a question. Is wallpaper hard to put up? I'm not very handy."

"It's easy," the clerk said. "Here is everything you need. This book tells exactly what to do. Now for the wallpaper. Do you like flowers? This lovely daisy pattern is on sale."

"I like it!" said Mr. Beetle. "I feel happy already. And it's the right price, too. I can't wait to get started."

Mr. Beetle read the instruction book as soon as he got home. "Hanging wallpaper is easy if you follow these directions. First, mix the paste. Wallpaper paste should not be watery or lumpy."

Mr. Beetle poured some water into a bucket. Then he added the powdered paste. The paste looked lumpy, so he added more water. But then it looked watery, so he added more paste. Then it looked lumpy again, so he added more water. Then more paste. What a mess! Finally, he got it right.

"Next, measure and cut the wallpaper. Spread the paste evenly on the back. Hang it on the wall. Be sure to smooth it out carefully."

Mr. Beetle measured and cut. He spread the paste evenly onto the back of the wallpaper. Then he got his ladder and climbed up to stick the wallpaper onto the wall. It stuck to the wall nicely. It stuck to Mr. Beetle nicely, too. Mr. Beetle's hands stuck to the wall. His feet stuck to the ladder. Mr. Beetle was stuck!

"Yoo-hoo! Mr. Beetle, are you home?"

It was his friend, Ms. Spider.

"Ms. Spider, help me! I'm in the living room!"

Ms. Spider came running. "Poor Mr. Beetle! How did you get so stuck?"

"It's this awful wallpaper! I'm throwing it away."

"Don't do that. It's such a pretty pattern. I can help. Let me hang it for you," Ms. Spider said.

"Do you know how?"

"Of course! It's easy." Ms. Spider got Mr. Beetle loose. Then she set to work. Ms. Spider worked fast. Soon she was done. Bright daisies burst from the walls of Mr. Beetle's living room.

"It's beautiful! How do you like it, Mr. Beetle?"

No answer.

"Mr. Beetle?" Ms. Spider looked all around. "I wonder where he went." Then she noticed a lump beneath the wallpaper. The lump was the size of a beetle. Ms. Spider gave it a poke.

"Help!" it said.

"Mr. Beetle! What are you doing underneath the wallpaper?" she asked.

"You work too fast. I couldn't get out of the way."

"I'm sorry, Mr. Beetle. I'll get you out." Ms. Spider went to fetch the scissors. Soon Mr. Beetle was free. He looked around the living room.

"It's beautiful! It looks like the most perfect day of summer."

"Yes it does," Ms. Spider said. "Now before this torn piece dries, I'll tear it off and replace it. Where is the rest of the wallpaper, Mr. Beetle?"

"Oh no! There isn't any more! What will I do?"

"I have an idea," Ms. Spider said. "May I borrow your paint box?"

Mr. Beetle brought his paint box. Ms. Spider removed the torn wallpaper. Then she carefully painted the bottom half of a Dutch door on Mr. Beetle's wall. Above it she painted a summer scene. Chickens pecked in the yard. Ducks swam in the pond. Cows grazed in the meadow, while a lark soared overhead in the sunshine.

"Look, Mr. Beetle. Instead of a wall, you have a door. Whenever the weather is dreary and cold, you can look out your door to a beautiful day.

You have your own summer day now, Mr. Beetle. A day of daisies and sunshine."

"Thank you, Ms. Spider," said Mr. Beetle. "Could I ask you another favor?"

"Of course!"

"Can you come by tomorrow? I would like to wallpaper the dining room."